In the Garden
Where Inspiration Grows

Deborah Morrison

Manor House

Library and Archives Canada
Cataloguing in Publication

Morrison, Deborah
In the garden : where inspiration grows / Deborah Morrison.

Poems.
ISBN 978-1-897453-27-8

I. Title.

PS8576.O7413I58 2009   C811'.6   C2010-900321-7

First Edition.
96 pages.

Cover design: Michael B. Davie and Donovan Davie

Special thanks to artist Lorraine Oberg for use of her cover
illustration: 'English Gardens'
Art courtesy of Lorraine Oberg, #21, 1752 Glastonbury Blvd.
N.W., Edmonton, Alberta, Canada, T5T 6W2.
Email: grebo@telusplanet.net   phone: 780-444-5704
Website: www.lorraineoberg.com

Published December 15, 2009
Manor House Publishing Inc.
www.manor-house.biz
(905) 648-2193

Manor House gratefully acknowledges the financial support of
the Government of Canada through the Book Publishing Industry
Development Program (BPIDP), Dept. of Canadian Heritage, for
our publishing activities.

*With love for my children,
Jared, Brandon and Leah Rose,
and my grandson Logan*

ACKNOWLEDGEMENTS

I express my sincere gratitude to my cherished family and friends who are truly inspiring.

I gratefully acknowledge editor and publisher Michael B. Davie for bringing the dream of this book to reality.

GUIDED MEDITATIONS:

The following are two series of powerful guided Meditations to activate your gifts of intentional imagination, inspiration and relaxation. The first, Entering the Garden guided meditations, bring you into a beautiful garden and are followed by a selection of your choosing from the more than 80 poems in this book: Vary them to create a series of guided meditations. The second, In the Garden series of guided meditations, take you deeper into the Garden; you can again vary selections of poems for a different meditation experience each time.

Entering the Garden guided meditations:

Make yourself comfortable either sitting or lying down. Close your eyes. Begin to focus your concentration on your breath. Inhale and exhale through the nose. Breathe slowly, effortlessly with deep abdominal breathing. Relax you entire body. Scan for any muscle tension, starting with your head and going all the way down to your toes. Take a deep breath and relax your entire body: head, shoulders, arms, hands, chest, abdomen, hips, legs, and feet. Now take a deep inhalation and as you exhale release any remaining tension in your body. You are now even more deeply relaxed.

Imagine yourself walking along a path through a beautiful green garden. The sun shining bright, filtered between the leaves... the birds are singing...the air is calm and warm.

As you walk along the path you come across an old gate. The gate creaks softly as you open it and you go through. You find yourself in a clearing... an overgrown garden... with beautiful flowers growing everywhere...vines climbing over stones…lush, green grass… and a sparkling, clear stream flowing gently along the far side of the clearing.

Breathe deeply, smell the flowers, listen to the birds…listen to the brook, clear and clean, as it tumbles over rocks…feel the gentle breeze warm against your skin… As you stroll, find a comfortable place to lay down on the emerald grass that glistens playfully in the golden sun. You watch the billowing white clouds drift slowly in the blue sky…you feel peaceful and calm…a perfect niche where you can feel completely relaxed…you feel content as you allow yourself to just enjoy the warmth and solitude of this peaceful place.

(At this point read aloud, or have recorded, a selection of poems of your choosing from this book)

It is now time to return… gently inhale and exhale as you slowly imagine yourself standing up with your feet firmly on the grass… It is now time to slowly come back to waking consciousness. Slowly move your fingers and toes, and then gently turn your head from side to side. When you are ready take three deep breaths, and open your eyes. You have returned.

In the Garden guided meditations:

Once again, make yourself comfortable either sitting or lying down. Close your eyes. Begin to focus your concentration on your breath. Inhale and exhale through the nose. Breath slowly, effortlessly with deep abdominal breathing. Relax you entire body. Scan for any muscle tension, starting with your head and going all the way down to your toes. Take a deep breath and relax your entire body: head, shoulders, arms, hands, chest, abdomen, hips, legs, and feet. Now take a deep inhalation and as you exhale release any remaining tension in your body. You are now even more deeply relaxed.

You are deep inside the Garden. As you relax on the green grass, you gently close your eyes and imagine a golden light entering through an opening in the crown of your head… the golden light flows down your head to your throat…experience the energy of the golden light and feel this vibrant energy as it flows down your arms, spine, legs, feet and down to your toes… feel and sense that wonderful feeling… glowing… melting… little rivulets of golden energy… feel a sensation of peace… and letting go… peace and letting go…

As you let go and relax, imagine a beautiful red rose bud at your heart centre… with each exhalation of your breath the rose bud begins to open…slowly…and unfolds as a beautiful, deep red rose…with a wonderful fragrance…as the petals open you notice the centre of the rose like a glowing crimson sky and the centre of the rose becomes brighter…the light spreads to the petals until the entire rose is glowing with radiant light.

You can feel the beauty of this wonderful rose…you can see the rose at your heart centre and the light from the rose is a brilliant, radiant energy of peace…a heightened vibration of wisdom, peace, and compassion… infinite, eternal glowing energy…bright with insight …contentment…know this radiant energy as the true centre of your being… know this beautiful light of wisdom and compassion as your ever present true nature… know that you can return to this peaceful, clear awareness of your heart centre whenever you want…it is always there, since this is the centre of your inner being, your true nature…a high vibration of healing love and light…

Take a few moments to silently enjoy this calm, abiding peace… breathe deeply and with each breath you feel more refreshed and rejuvenated. You feel good as you allow yourself to just enjoy this peaceful awareness.

You know that you have received the positive energy you need to clear and balance emotions, relieve stress and release limitations…as you create a clear powerful connection to your Higher Self you joyfully open your heart and allow miracles to unfold…envision your abundance manifest now… take a few moments to silently enjoy this wonderful connection to your Higher Self…

(At this point read aloud, or have recorded, a selection of poems of your choosing from this book)

It is now time to return… gently inhale and exhale as you slowly imagine yourself standing up with your feet firmly on the grass…you hear the softly babbling brook as you turn to walk toward the old gate at the edge of the Garden… your awareness of a joyful peace is radiant throughout your entire being; the garden and the rose at your heart centre are crystal clear…you decide to leave this secret retreat for now… and yet, you know that you may visit this special place whenever you wish.

It is now time to slowly come back to waking consciousness. Slowly move your fingers and toes, and then gently turn your head from side to side.

When you are ready take three deep breaths, and open your eyes. You have returned.

INNER SUN

Sphere of gold is rising
dawn enlightens
Earth and Heaven awaken
consciousness unfolds morning's blessing
gives birth to a new day
deeper we journey into the light
to our inner spark Divine

Mid-day golden orb plays
high in the Heavens, gathers
morning mist and afternoon shadows
weaves them into high noon
infused with wisdom's brilliance
cosmic convergence
bright with universal force
infinite mingles with finite
nexus, where Earth and Heaven
lovingly embrace, warm
with soft shimmering radiance

Amber sun is setting
Supersoul of all creation
cosmic centre of Love, Truth
we rejoice, intoxicated with
inner peace
Heaven and earth kiss
Sun melts into the horizon
joins heart to heart
soul to Soul

Silver moon playfully rises
in reflections of Sun's light
Heaven's night whispers
his song of silence
Stars dance in the stillness, Earth is
bathed in her moon's heavenly light
joins Life to life in Love's
blissful emanations of Inner Sun

FANTASY

Classical sonatas, streams of
fantasies
intoxicating, enchanting
evokes a vision
of twin candle flames
their fire a light of passion
a poetic reverie
we revel in
subtle glance
spontaneous
moon-swept eyes

strings sing of romance
song of the soul
rapture, anguish of love

now only memories embrace
my moments with you
I won't tell of the willow in the mist
near the girl in jeans, a deeper shade of worn
with melody sublime our paths meander
near water's melodious ripples
then fade
near the shore…
I'm left
in amorous wandering
longing for more…

DREAMS IN A GARDEN

I stand 'midst lilies
and wisteria
to ponder... I see
the horizon, sea touches sky
a vision merges
into my soul
like a gentle spring rain
penetrating into the
depths of earth
absorbed by roots
of being
flowers
into a garland
gives meaning
to all that passes
yet forever eludes
full apprehension
petals unfold with
elegance, symmetry, of
wondrous possibilities...
yet the greatest
of present realities...the moment...
I touch the soft petal
of a burgundy rose
and feel the infinite
at the heart
of my garden,
...timelessness...

SOLITUDE

The path is silvery with branches evergreen
as I wander among their designs
interlacing of shadow and sunlight
the breeze warm, playful, softened by such
sweetened fragrance
Lily of the valley, wild violet
become symbols of my heart's despair
intermingling scents and colours, stirring memories long
asleep
of a time we walked together, hands held close
dreaming our forever, now shattered into a mosaic
darkness and light, fire and ice
joy and sorrow brought to mind
reawakens deeper understanding
filling me with love, I entrust myself to
Life, breath, and thought
that there are no destinations
only spinning wheels of time
seasons passing and ever ending
bring new beginning, a woven fate,
a tapestry of tears and laughter, ever changing,
thus on a pathway etched with dreams and memories
and with fragrant scent imbued,
I discover my Sacred Self, bow in prayer and
raise my heart in wondrous solitude

NEXUS

Vast as infinity
mysterious as the star filled skies
universally paradoxical
reaches high into the heavens
yet deeper and deeper still
to oceans depths
a brilliance that brings
warmth to our shores
with our skies ablaze
sets us on our journey
the greatest one of all
a discovery of the still point
our centre, at the heart of
us together
spark of the heavens
fire of the soul
universal
nexus

REALITY

Dawn
expands, uplifts
light enters darkness…
in joy I dance, with heightened awareness
take the next leap
land from the air on
new ground, unique
a great mirror… reveals
reflections of myself, I discover
the key…

I only go outward to get further
inside, and I only get further
when I know the revelations
of my intuition, live
their reflections
in the external world

I hold a lavender bouquet
of Cosmos softly in my hand
remember that life is an
interactive mirror of internal
and external realities,
dancing in holographic
interplay

TO LOVE A BLUEBELL

Walking by my garden one night
I saw a bluebell, a serene sight at dusk
"I love this bluebell and possess I must
I want this bluebell and possess I will"
thus I drew near my magnificent bluebell
my ego brilliant, my hand reached out
caressing emerald leaves, kissing petals blue,
joyous would it be in my grasp
loved and cherished, free from storms
is it love to remove my bell so blue?
heavens! Overcome with sorrow
my bluebell now more blue than ever!
'alas, what is it to truly love...
who knows what it is to love...
save me from storms to rest in your arms,
what hypocrisy, to satisfy desire!'
scorned, my bluebell closed his petals
'The garden is a part of me and I of them,
if you love me then let me be
hold me in your heart,
nurture with memories,
for love that's ever true
ever knows
true longing

BLEEDING HEARTS

My aunt's head rests on my shoulder
weary, in need of solace
her one and only daughter
at rest in a rose covered casket
my cousin, little golden haired one
with eyes of sapphire blue
as tears, then more tears
fall with overwhelming grief
so young
yet it was her time…
my arms reach out, my heart breaks
all over again, wanting only
to offer a place of comfort
a moment of reassurance
in our sorrow's depths
our only peace is in knowing
her daughter lives on
in our hearts, that
she has found her peace,
we will always
remember her
and send her our
wishes
of love

FORGET-ME-NOT

Spellbound by love
I dream a lover's dream
just as radiant light
of morning star is thrown
you fill my soul with
splendour sublime
released from love's shadows
into the stillness
you carry me
to a world beyond
the wonder of the sun
where moonlight and love
mingle into one
glorious rhapsody

PASSION FLOWER

Flirting with fire my
sultry seducer
dripping with nectar, as
passion flowers
I surrender to my
fascination
of you

SEEDS AND YEARNINGS OF THE SOUL

Memories, emotions and images
cosmic connection
intimacy between
consciousness and soul
I bask in visions
without expectation
enveloped in a world
of imagination,
essence
of my soul
each moment is artwork…
reveals expression
of inner wonder
my soul sings
envisions
freedoms, destinies
in the glow of passionate life
I bring a creative edge
to every action and
empower each moment with possibility…
inner essence is the seed
that empowers my
being as depths
of mystery bring my soul
to life…

REFLECTION

Time moves
more slowly here
my soul
is at home
in this wondrous place
a botanical, creative
space
hidden, mysterious, free
I am enticed
to slow down
in this garden
exquisitely
enclosed by a solid
stone wall
with a strong
iron gate
I breathe in beauty
of liminal space
charm adorns
this wonderful place
delicately balanced
between
nature and culture
where artistic, creative
arrangements flower
as more important
than striving for profit
my innermost heart
is expressed
restored

CHERRY BLOSSOSM

In
my garden
sitting down
forgetting
everything

freeing
my imagination
to wonder in fruitful
reverie

steady
I sit
beneath my pink
cherry blossom
tree

without
wavering I
am inviting
soul
in

ENCHANTED

I see the alchemy of light
reflections on the icy chaos
in cascades of April storm
I hear the numinous in nature's
wild, furious symphony of snow
such brilliance charms me,
I touch reflections of silver moon
shadows play on this
silver snowy scene,
I feel a spark of the eternal
like diamonds at play
in frozen drifts of ice,
this awe -inspiring waterfall
of crystal gems
fills the depths
of my heart and soul,
I know Divinity resides
in all
I am enchanted

AN ODE TO MY WHISPERING WILLOW

In the searing summer heat
mysterious Moon hidden yet near
dwell not in that fiery inferno
soon cooling light will emanate forth
reveal subtle radiance as dusk appears
envelope limbs of emerald
with an ode of amorous song
devotions will we sing unto each other
the Whispering Willow and
the Summer Moon
together will shine
in song ever more

FOR MY SPRING STREAM

I discover this day
where you are a stream
and I am the moon
we melt ourselves into
a rare and perfect reflection
rippled light in waves of
ever changing surfaces
ebb and flow
we splash lyrical verse everywhere
poetry does spring forth unto each other…
for it is the heart of the poet
that truly knows how to love

SUN AND MOON

In the cool of the night
moon is longing for sun
dwell not so far away
from my loving embrace
we two are soul mates
destined,
crafted of one fire
enlighten the self same earth
our home we ever share
infinite vastness of deep eternal sky
come closer I'll kiss you
at dusk on the horizon
tell you secrets of my soul
feel your warmth
eclipse
time
and
space

A FLOWER

If I planted a flower
every time I thought of you
then we would have a
garden that we
could walk in forever

MY SONG OF SILENCE

To the Wind hushed
in the depths
of my garden
silent I await
miraculous Wind
when he sings
blue Summer Moon
will whisper
of summers to come
as we lift
our hearts
in the poetics
of dance

MOTHER EARTH AND FATHER SKY

In golden drops of dawn
kisses of emerald dew
musings of a poetess
harmonies of celestial song
complementarities of artist's brush
in Divine embrace they
play in creations of the day
She is upheld in His infinite vastness
while He lives in Her as
She dwells within
His eternal embrace
absorbs His wondrous presence
His falling rain
melting snow
morning sun
Mother Earth and Father Sky
balance and enhance
each within the other
together they co-create
universal
poetic
harmony

ALCHEMY

Encircled by indigo twilight
dusk in my garden
reflecting on my dreams
summer breeze warm
gently plays with
bells on my walking stick,
transforms my despair into hope
my weary soul begins to warm,
what I had seen as obstacles
were actually great old trees
dancing in the wind
the usual song of the cardinal now gone
just beautiful setting sun
after new fallen rain
all this movement, yet so still
bells softly play, yet so quiet
and the warm, this wondrous warm,
what a gift,
as I wander along
dodging deep shadows
or anything else that could bring me discomfort,
I experience the profound cadence
of my garden;
with time this authenticity,
this cadence, mysterious
alchemy of garden land,
brings new vitality
transforms everything it touches,
into beautiful

SYMPHONY OF BLUE

The mystery of a garden
of light and birth revealed
I feel my soul in harmony
with the spirit of the earth,
from within this magnificent landscape
is revealed the wonder of life
summer's silhouetted abundance
Irises and Peonies abound
splash their many colours of
enlightened age- old wisdom,
summer's destiny is
to expand life
ever changing, never ending images
cast by a kaleidoscopic magnifying glass
larger and larger, artful design
until life bursts forth
radiant,
in a seed,
a flower,
a sun,
in a star,
in my
heart…

ETCHED

Intricate scarlet designs weave summer
botanicals on a tapestry of soft earthen brown
ruby red poppies peak proud, etched erubescence
across the yielding terrestrial field
two free butterflies alight on crimson petal softness
like drifting clouds of daydreams become
manifest artful designs, horticultural miracles
emerge from solar drenched soil
golden orb enlightens, shimmering beams
sizzle shades of emerald aesthetics
like gems that catch the sun
adorn elegant trees,
leaves, grasses, while their tangled roots
descend deeper underground
into the sultry mid-day soil
Mother Earth's embrace is alchemy
like a Sacred Temple

FALLING RAIN

Prolific streams descend
falling gentle rain
liquid love trickles
fulfills thirsty yearning roots
energizes young seedlings
art emerging from struggle
new creation, an act of rebellion
against parched clay
this illicit act transcends the mundane
everyday status quo
to balance preservation
with creation,
life escapes present manifest structure
perfect symmetry springs from
emerging celebrations
of new life

SONG OF THE GARDEN

If you created Earth's abundant gardens
planted infinite stars and
set the universe into wondrous motion
would you care for a weary heart's dreams
or the tears of a sorrowful child
if you traversed across time and space
beyond boundaries we perceive
with eternity's rose in your hand
would your awareness encompass
every heartbeat, count each breath
measure the grains of sand
knowing all of the hand spun strands
of this great universal design together
weave this vast cosmic dream

The strands are the tapestry
as the tapestry is the strands,
each blade of grass
to a star is aligned,
holds the melody of Mother Earth,
echoes the legend of Father Sky

SANCTUARY

Shades of pink transform nebulous gloom into the first
blush of rose
uplift soaring spirit higher,
                    where we are healed
and in this rose garden become one
where artistically crafted wooden beams
surround us like a temple
in this open-air gazebo we stand
profuse vines climb and roots descend
heart, mind, body and soul entwine
within a handcrafted masterpiece

With sandals we cross paths
traverse through this vast garden
abundant with treasure,
                    enfolded in peace
the making of our temenos shared,
a certain spirit breathes life
                    into our footsteps,
imprints of the sacred,
                    dimensions of aesthetics
the spiritual richness of simplicity,
some rocks skilfully placed
                    imply wall and form
create a fountain that overflows
                    with inspiration

Lilies, Foxglove, Delphinium, Cosmos, Roses abound
surround us as far as the eye can see
we are enshrined, reconcile fundamental
                                    dimensions
of this experience, as our attention is
                             lifted
in stages from Earth to Heaven
our wandering in the Aviary, Herb Garden,
Lover's garden is sacred play

Such joy shelters our soul,
                  garlands us
with safekeeping, housed in this
                  botanical mansion
rich with memory, keeping and caring
we take the time to cherish the flowers
hold each other's spirit softly,
                  graced with enchantment

THE HEALER

Into the herb garden she walks
bare feet silent on cool paths of flagstone
with a hand-woven wicker basket by her side
she gathers leaf, root and flower
ingredients for healing and potpourri

Lavender's wonderful autumnal scent
sachets sweet to perfume clothes
infused in water to soothe aches, bring calm

Rosemary, a traditional herb of friendship, remembrance
in ancient times believed to strengthen memory
its name means sea dew, has amatory associations

Thyme is delightful, sweet, attractive to bees
Wild Thyme honey, marvellous in flavour
traditionally the flowers must be gathered
near the side of the hill where fairies used to be

Basil is aromatic, indispensable in cookery
Rue was once known as the herb of grace
Bergamot is fragrant with bright red flowers
Nettle grows tall, a medicinal herbal
Elder with flowers to make wine, berries for jam, syrup
Camomile for tea to ward off colds, soothe the nerves

Each flower, leaf, root of every clime
she gathers in the dewy morning
fills her basket high for making herbal medicine
concoctions, infusions, teas, aromatherapy,
Bach flower remedies, scented oils,
Homeopathic, and dried flower artistry

MY HOME

My home one day will be
with walls made of huge solid stones,
a grand bay window, sunlight shining through
a double chimney with billowing cedar scented smoke
a cosy hearth for warmth from the crackling fire
the vaulted ceiling high with great wooden beams
huge clay pots with Ivy, Impatience,
Fuscia, Begonia and Lobelia,
Foxglove growing tall near the front door,
an ancient Chinese Cherry tree
shades the grasses below near the
garden full with crimson Roses and
Lilies bright with their showy oranges and yellows
nestled among the Delphinium serene
there is room by the back garden fence
for many climbers, bushes of Rose
colourful whites, yellows, reds, pinks
fragrant Lilac, Black-Eyed-Susan
near bushes with flowers of snow white
the Yucca grows tall, stately
surrounded with Fern's shades of green,
garden is poetry of the earth and
my dream home one day will be
built on a solid foundation from
poetics
of the soul

DREAMS COME TRUE

When bees gather nectar
from fiery red orange Lupine flowers
and deep purple Irises
bloom in the heart of summer
to my secret place I wander, taste
the honey sweetness of what has been
what can be
my mind becomes still, free
visions clear, images of possibility
are born from life's creative balance
destiny, freewill, faith, hope;
to times afar my feelings stir
of new, happier days
for contentment like honey's sweeteners
is gathered over time's many seasons
from cherished dreams that come true
along the way

MY ROSE

Dance

        in summer breeze

happiness

        beauty

           grace

heart opens

        to blessings

joy enlivens

        contentment

           flowers...

IN THE GARDEN

In the garden Daisies lift their faces to the sun
with petals pearl white and butter yellow,
lacy edged Iris of pink, soft cream
grow into the light, Lilies search upward
grow higher in brilliant free-flowing style,
violet Roses of soft rich velvet lift their hearts
to mid-day's golden orb, Hollyhocks sway, dance
higher toward the bright,
if we turn away from shadows
like flowers,
we'll see
only
light

WILD ROSES

Make my mind still as a calm lake without waves
thoughts clear as crystal water
by your grace open my heart softly
like petals of a wild Rose
scent my words with your sweet inspiration
let all my cares drift into the mists
that I may share your ways of wisdom,
for that which grows wild, free
is always more beautiful
than that which is cultivated,
may creative, natural, spontaneity
be the still small voice
that guides my way
in humble gratitude
I arise to your sacred ways
oh Great Spirit
source Eternal

DAFFODIL

The meandering path
to our destiny is
like a butterfly
here, there, everywhere
until depth and higher meaning
is discovered from within
then with wings open
guided to one glorious Daffodil
a soul fulfilled with purpose
uplifted with
passion over rationality
heart before head
faith over reason

BE YOURSELF

The Crocus grows in its own way
close to the ground
opens at its own pace
early in spring
chooses its rightful place
scattered through grasses,
this humble, simple flower
is content with its uniqueness
like the Crocus be who you are
nurture your dreams
live with authenticity
a self fully expressed
remember that in a world
where you can be anything
just be yourself

MIRACLES

You have an inner power
believe in your own potential
like the honey bee
by following your own path
your destiny will flower
each day take wing
discover awesome, magnificent beauty
in the world and within yourself
just as the bee discovers nectar
amaze yourself with the sweet possibilities
of each new day

SELF CONFIDENCE

45

Be like the Lilac
show your true colours
with positive thinking
focus, concentrate
on creating happiness
stay balanced in body
         calm in heart
         strong in spirit
         clear in mind
there is so much you
have to offer
never become lost
in self doubt
live with self-confidence
celebrate your marvellous strengths

AMARYLLUS

With uplifted spirit
live your happiness
let joy reflect
in what you do
your special qualities
have carried you this far
overcome adversity by looking
on the bright side
work things out
one step at a time
stay near to those
who sincerely care
show the world
who you really are
hold onto your dreams
never let them go

A LIFE OF HAPPINESS

Like the Moonflower
grow high and well rounded
love with all of your soul
with your entire being
your true happiness
comes from within
find your joy in
everything you do
be in relationships
worthy of all that you are
be aware of what you like
and what is not so appealing
be mindful of choosing goals carefully
you will get only
that which you seek
like the Moonflower
create one of a kind
beauty in life

NEST FULL OF EGGS

Believe in your own power
enjoy the magnificence
of just being alive
each day discover wondrous beauty
in the world, look with hope
today is what we truly have
be open to your own power
your own potential
embrace your inner force
come out of your shell
possibilities can become
miracles

MIXED FLOWERS

Every day is like a mixed bouquet
of rewards and unique challenges
life is shaped with great variety
a mixed garden of flowers
we create our worlds
by our thoughts, words and deeds
we can change, re-arrange
we can decide how far
how fast we desire to go
endless changes, our days, a mixed garden
rich with colour, texture, growth,
we can create each day
like landscape designers
balance light, shade and form
like gardeners plant seeds
of aspirations and
by gardening discover
who we really are

VIEW FROM ABOVE

Stand high
take a view from above
see that in our power we can
live a life with true meaning
envision living life
one day at a time
by cherishing each moment
being grateful for each day
living life to the fullest
then one day we see it has
all come together
our hopes have finally
come
to be

DESIGNS OF DESTINY

Listen to your own heart
from deep within you know your way
plant your own dreams
design your destiny
you are free, unlimited
every moment, each day
be all you can be
create beauty along the way
your life has a purpose
you have great power
so reach out
      make a difference
           let you imagination
                soar

52

PATHWAY

The pathway to a dream
sometimes paved with challenges, changes
failure and trying again and again
along the way you may experience
difficulties, setbacks
obstacles to withstand
conquer your path with each step
walk with courage and faith
continue with persistence
until you reach the end
where your dream has come true
there is no greater happiness

IRIS

Is there a beautiful dream in your heart
wonderful, lovely as a summer flower
remember that failure cannot
destroy your dreams
that dedication and years
of work have built
just believe in yourself
water your dreams
help them grow
with patience and hope
a bright tomorrow is near
keep believing, after each dark night
a new sun rises
dreams come true and
like the Iris
reveal their beauty

PEONY

Know what you like
who you want to be
creatively express
your feelings,
view the world
with sensitivity
be true to yourself
and everyone else
follow your heart
live your wisdom
in your own way,
like a Peony, your dreams
will blossom
with beauty and grace

CLEMATIS

Clematis has reached a wooden wall
with its support grows strong and tall
may your roads traveled have blessings
that, like the wall, also give you comfort to grow
may time be abundant
sunshine plentiful
with rains that nourish
quiet and gentle
with friends that share laughter
family that give love
may your dreams be in reach
remember all of your good fortune
be thankful on your journey and
for your future
may the stars be in reach

DAHLIA

I give you a Dahlia
that I grew in my garden
I give you a promise
that I'll always be true
remember who I am
hold onto my hopes
reach out for the stars
live with happiness
do the things
we want to do,
being true to ourselves,
together we can enjoy life,
day by day
helping each other
tend our gardens
growing lives of
love and joy

HOLLYHOCK

The pattern of life grows, is beautiful,
like the glorious Hollyhock
you may wonder about
the direction that life has taken
rather than being lost in confusion
be calm, accept the path
before you now
walk proud and cast
your dreams to the stars
soon your steps will become sure
the path become comfortable
you will discover experiences
never imagined, believe in yourself
let your spirit soar

HYDRANGEA

There are no boundaries
to what you can be
no limits to what
life might offer you
the world is filled
with as many possibilities
as you are full of potential
be open and embrace
the wonder of experience
believe in the richness of
yourself

LILY

Lily, You are the flower
of Gabriel, the angel of hope
you are a song
that makes my heart sing,
deep feeling that shows me
what I must do
help me find what
I am looking for
You are the wisdom within
leading to my destiny
You are life's harmony,
As I listen to Your song
I become who
I was always meant to be
complete, happy,
at peace

BUTTERFLY

Like the butterfly
free
to fly high
on wings of gold
rejoice in peace
on leaves so green
appears as essence of beauty
with song of silence
wandering spontaneously
being a flutter of inspiration
soul
    inner
        Truth

SUNFLOWER

Have you ever
grown something
in the garden
of your mind...
think about things
then the ideas will grow
imagination
is the seed
of creativity
like the Sunflower
reach to the light
discover infinite
possibility

POND

Placid
cool
in summer's scorching fire
surface ever calm
waters running deep
serene, clear reflections
of golden light beyond
a soothing oasis in
midst of a sandstorm
such ever present stillness quenches
the depths of my being
may the entire world attain
peace

ECHINACEA

Healing flowers are magic
grown from the depths
of my garden
soul medicine
with energies of illumination

Echinacea enables us
to heal life forces
strengthen the immune system
restore inner balance
naturally

BUTTERFLY ON BUSH

You ask why I make my home
adrift from leaf to leaf
I smile and I am silent
my soul in peace is quiet,
the flowers blossom
the waters flow
while I take flight
as in a beautiful dream
from one illumination to
another

TREASURE

Soulful rush
crystal stream
evanescent
powerful
clear sound rejuvenates
life's mysterious flow

majestic emerald willow
magnificent, ever weeping
heart's song dancing
my eyes pour
deep indigo
on grasses beneath
yet beauty thrusts at
my spirit
awakens dreams,
memories, carefree
I walk across coolness
of steady stone bridge
feel rock solid strength
sun flashes bright
into my eyes,
thunder of water voices
call to me

I surrender
I wander near
effervescent waters
rushing over soaring cliff
pouring millions of diamonds
like blessings,
                sparkle,
                        cascade
to
        Earth's
                upheld
                        hands

AUTUMN'S CHOREOGRAPHY

In morning's stillness
wind blown gold and amber,
freed autumn jewels descend
bring tree's greatness down to earth
crack of bare branches
crunch of brown leaves
buries last grasses, walkways,
fallen flower

Sunrise bursts into hope
of ground covered embrace
protection from snow's deep chill

aspects of autumn's choreography
humble earthen blankets of compassion

LIFE'S KITE

Spring breeze flows free
I grasp tighter to a silken string
attached to my kite, flying
higher now with steadiness,

The Eternal keeps watch over all
She holds dear in Her hands the
string of my life's kite

Today She pulls the string taut
tomorrow She'll leave it loose

Yet I'm sure the string is
ever in Her hands

FALL

Set free the last leaf
falls toward earthen brown softness
liberated forever from attachment
to the great tree of life
letting go completely
swirling, twirling deeper
drifting joyous with absolute
faith in gentle breezes of Eternity
with total surrender
into the loving arms
of Mother Earth

WE TWO ARE ONE

Icy pearls on branches glisten
in praise of Your great light
drifts like opals piled high
adorn Your brilliance
ivory flakes, round, full
fall into wondrous white
gazing on soft-fallen splendour
I merge into winter's beauty
become one with You

in stillness the silence
pillows my weary soul

We two are One, steadfast
unchangeable, awake in
Your sweet sublime artistry
I look to the night's dark
heavens, as a bright star
shines forth in
miraculous grace

and even yet
from the very depths
of my heart
I feel
reflections
of Your omnipresence...

Still,
    still
to 'hear' Your
tender breath brush
gentle on my cheek
and so to know the warmth
of You
within this snowy
wintry night

WINTER WIND

The winter wind blows
and restless is my spirit
even my feet of clay
beg direction
yet cold days pass and pass
one just like the next
leaving my weary soul unfulfilled,
yearning for the warmth
of summer's blessing

my love waits quietly in silence
I know not where...

not even one compass can I find
to guide my next step
north or south, east or west
this icy day closes in upon me
I am surrounded by snow's white void,
frost's mysterious, empty designs
I am drowning in this
frozen ocean of nothingness, one day
my longing will gather its own power
like the stream that has reached the sea
then I will come back to you

UNDER TWILIGHT'S SILVER MOON

Was it only yesterday
that we met in a dream

I hear your song in my solitude

with my longing for you
I have built a castle in the clouds
yet today the clouds drift apart

rising from our slumber we find
ourselves at noon in tomorrow's new day
our dream is over and yet
we are only half awake
we wonder why we must part while
the new day overflows with its own fullness

in the dusk of our memories
if the clouds once again come together under
twilight's silver moon
we will meet once more
and again speak together

you will sing to me a deeper song
we will meet in a new dream
if in this 'dream' our hands touch in loving embrace
then another castle we will build
in the twilight of summer's
warm clear sky

FOR THIS

For this I remember you most
that You give so lovingly to me
yet do not know that You give at all
my Beloved, Your kindness soothes my soul
Your loving, tender ways are my balm
become my tomorrow's blessing
today I sit alone on the hill-top
gazing down on the valley below
I can see you ever more clearly
from this great distance
my Beloved, even when you are far,
I realize that You are closer than ever
from this great height
in winter's solitude, the secret of my joy
is to know that we are never
ever really apart

A DEEPER THIRST

My Beloved, You are like the ocean
vast, deep, strong,
I see only the good in You
together we are like waves
from a memory long ago
love in quest of Love
You ease my deeper thirst for life
there is no greater gift to give
You are my life's fountain
my parched lips are quenched
whenever I come to You to drink
I find You also thirsty

then we drink of one another
fulfilled in both giving and receiving

MY BELOVED

you are sweet my beloved
sweeter than laughter
greater than my longing for You
I adore your boundless vastness
your song is a chant
my heart throbs as I listen
I behold the Eternal in you and
love you, such love can reach
any distance in this vast universe
the Eternal binds us to our destiny
where we find and cherish one another
you give me a rose and together we are
lifted into heaven's joy

IN TIMES DESTINED

My days were brief with you
the words we spoke but few
in summer's glory your voice
faded from my ears
yet your love never vanished
from my memory
I will come again to you
you will find me with a
richer soul, a heart pouring over
unto you, and I will speak to
your spirit, though many days may
hide me, and a great silence enfolds us
I will seek you once again
bring you sweet Lily of the Valley
I will not seek in vain

love will reveal itself
in a deeper, more clear voice
in words that ring true
in times destined
for heart and soul

TWO SEEDS

Now it is evening my beloved
I wander alone in my summer garden
the earth sleeps
yet I remain awake thinking of you

we two are like seeds of one plant
in our ripeness we experience
a fullness of heart

the summer wind blows and
we are cast adrift on waves of breezes
blown apart in summer's heat

freed, unencumbered, I long
only for you
my beloved

MY FREEDOM

Have I spoken of anything else

all my reflection is of You
neither thought, word, or deed
will make me forget You
surprised I wonder at the
ever springing of my soul
even while my hands
plant the seeds, and tend my garden
who else can spend her hours
so immersed in visions of You
You are a part of my soul, my body
even the wind and the sun
will never tear us apart

my freedom comes through
remembering You
from dawn
to dawn

MY SOUL ENCHANTED

At night I remember You
and hope that I will
see You in the rise of the dawn
at noon I wonder if I have seen
You walking in the garden
toward the sunset
in winter's high snow
I wonder if You'll come in spring
running through rolling hills of wildflower
in summer heat I almost thought
I saw You dancing in the Autumn leaves
in the fall I thought You came to me
with a design of frost in Your hair
my heart is enflamed and my soul enchanted
You are my ecstasy

NEVER APART

Where shall I seek You and
how shall I find You
but to be myself and
consult with my higher Spirit
how will I speak of You
except through song
You are a passionate beauty
like the tempest You
shake the stars above
You are a soft whispering
that speaks to my spirit
I quiver as I sense your presence
I have heard You in my garden,
in the forest and near the stream
with my cries I heard the sound of You
like the mystery of a vast silence
in the stillness I ask in my heart
how will we ever be together
You are my need and my ecstasy
then You answer me
with fullness of heart,
affirming that
we have never,
ever really
been
apart

RULES OF THE GARDEN

Rules
made to be broken, it is good
to know and understand them
flowers in efficient straight lines
yet
be not content to leave the matter there
know all the rules
but break them whenever needed
let a wild thing grow
that is what makes life's garden
so constantly unexpected, enthralling
be not hidebound by rules
become a supreme artist and
discover true originality
true art breaks all rules
what would have become of my garden
if
  I had chased
          rules
              instead of

                 n
              o
            i
          t
       a
      r
     i
    p
   s
  n
i

GARDEN OF SPRING

Here the white robed Rose is born,
Peony spring, and the buttered Tulip;
And Daffodil in their puffed emerald slip,
Pallet their colour 'round every budding thorn,
Lively blooms leave the winter's chill outworn.
Here too the gliding Robin has her nest,
Enclosed in blue-hued stone walls; flowers adorn,
Luscious Delphinium sway in dance on soft crest,
In shade of a near bough, miraculous song!
A silence deep from this botanical peace,
And these fair emerald stems that climb and throng,
This exuberant world of colourful seas,
Of flowing life, and soul adrift in breeze,
Each wondrous blossom abounds with
Precious more splendor
            Than these!

PEOPLE OF PEACE

They reflect and express
The beauty of the human spirit
In us all

They transform conflict into
Conversations of compassion,
Understanding common bonds

They know our shared desires,
To live in harmony and happiness,
They know our dreams for peace

They guide the world
From illusion and misguided notions,
Freeing our inner potential

That aggression, violence and war,
That exploitation of the weak,
And lack of freedom with forced control,
Lead to nothing but destruction

They understand that to destroy
One of us, standing next to us,
Or living a world away,
Is to destroy Mother Earth
In the disregard of Her giving

They are aware that greed
For Her resources
Is to destroy the future of our living planet

They guide the world
From the mind and spirit
And heart of kindness

They understand the paths of peace
As the only path worth traveling,
That any other path leads to
No destination at all that
Any of us truly want to go

Who are they…they are the people of peace,
And people of peace are the treasure of
Mother Earth

THE WAY IS CLEAR

There was a time when
I focused on discipline
Then after a while I learned
To emphasize sincerity

There was a phase of my life
When I desired attainment
Yet with passing of time
I've come to cherish wisdom

Now I emphasize wisdom's
True function as compassion
Of self and others

Once I tried to find
Absolute answers yet
Rather than answers
I now emphasize the truth,
Wonder and mystery
Of this precious life
Just as it is

Rather than transcendence
And perfect enlightenment
I focus on a simple life
Of spontaneous original faith

And the daily practice
Of clarity, joy and peace

There was a time when
I wondered where peace was
And went in search for it
Everywhere

Now the way is clear
And I know the key
To true peace
Is held within the very depths
Of our hearts

I realize we're always free
To choose how much peace we'll create
How much peace we'll share
In living each and every
Precious day

I AM HERE

I am here
In the early morning
In the searing summer sun
At the summit of each day

I am here
Searching for
The one and only you
Wanting to look deep in your eyes
Finding your soul vibrant and bright
Like the flame of a candle

I am here
When dusk plays
Between darkness and light
On top of the mountain
In our temple of dreams

I am here
Whenever you remember me,
Sit down beside me
Where only we can go

I am here
For you, a tree to shelter you
Soul within soul
I'm always with you

A SACRED PEACE

The Rose
Speaks to us
Of wholeness
The totality
Of creation

The Rose
Not separate from
The stars, or the moon
In one instant
Can bring me into
The timeless present

Lost in wonder
I remember
The earth
That holds such beauty
As a Rose,
Beauty of
The earth
Expressed in flowers…

Imagine
From fallen leaves
This earth is enriched
To nourish growth,
Life…

I envision
A sacred peace,
This circle of
Life…seasons…
That go on
Forever…

THE CLARITY OF ESSENCE

I see that no fierce clarity
Cares to manifest
Enmeshed by reflections, wrapped in mist
I ponder the obscure,
Hidden by it's own inherent nature
By frustration of life's finite, restrictive severity
I try to hold onto the mist in my hands
As if it were earth

Yet I realize that to sharpen
Beyond five senses, I must
Mind this moment here
Awaken to always subtle new and now
As I let go in surrender
I feel the brilliant
White-capped waves
Rhythmically caressing the shore
This mist can but enhance
Dawn's symphony of light

I see it all around and within, mist
That defines this endless morning sky
No lighthouse though
To guide my soul
On voyages free of maps or charts
Spontaneous awareness
Not concrete formula, but art

When my eye within sees
A mysterious essence
Like a tiny water drop
That lovingly has merged
Into the ocean
So intimate they embrace eternity
Then I come to know
An aspect of myself
Beyond time and space

I BELIEVE

I give you a white Rose in surrender
And tell you of deepest thoughts…
I believe it is not necessary
To fight or argue in relationship
And that all differences and
Disagreements can be resolved
By open, non-blaming, loving
Discourse

I give you a yellow Rose for strength
And tell you of inner qualities…
I believe in equality, harmony that is on
All levels, a gentle and peaceful
Balance

I give you a pink Rose of affection
And share my true feelings…
I believe in living with a deep, sensual
Passion that is like an ever
Present undercurrent based on
Openness, honesty, trust,
Communication, integrity
Fearlessness

I give you a red Rose in sincerity
And tell of lasting love…
I believe in union, a creative
Meeting on all levels
To the very core of our
Being

I give you a violet Rose of hope
And tell you of dreams…
I believe in us
Together
Creating a world
Of kindness, joy and
Peace

LOVE'S MYSTERIES

Love's mysteries drift
In crystal waters of emerald green
Beneath the surface of a turbulent sea
In the silent wishes of dreamers

Moments together appear like grains of sand
In depths of the sea
Yet waves of time cast
These grains adrift

We seek to wander
Beneath cloudless skies
Let truth reveal itself
In heavens of clear blue

With each grain of sand
That ebbs and lows
In our sea of dreams
Deep emotions stir our hearts

So many stars in the quiet sky
Their light reveals hidden truth, like pearls
Once floating beneath the surface
Now shimmering in the darkness
Along starlit shores

OUR LOVE

Our love
So sweet, sublime
Reaches beyond time

Embraces our
Souls, spins the Earth
With each hope and dream

Shadows are
Cast on our days apart
Lost between the clouds

Our love
Of light and inspiration
Reaches among the heavens

Yet our love so strong, intoxicating
Is
Like a chalice of nightshade

Our fate
Of life ever apart
Written in the stars

*** UNTITLED ***
By Leah Rose Morrison

Compassion soars out from her,
Like a white dove,
Gracefully touching all her children's hearts.

Radiant light dances around us,
Darkness is no longer,
We can all see the way.

She is a calm pond,
Filled with lotus flowers,
Washing away all our fears.

She is an elegant sunrise,
Colourful,
Inspiring our hopes and dreams.

She is a wise willow tree,
Protecting us from the rain,
Branches dancing playfully around us,
Offering shade.

She is the sun,
Ever bright and full of life,
Making our world warm and joyful.

She is a simple piece of paper,
A place to let go of all our thoughts and ideas,
Always accepting whatever we write,
Forever listening.

She is the wind,
Strong and powerful,
Changing everything it touches,
Helping us to be lifted toward the sky.

She is a soft pillow,
A place to rest our minds,
Comforting,
Safe.

She is a good book,
Offering advice and new ideas,
Sharing with us endless knowledge.

She is everywhere,
In my heart,
No matter where I am,
What I'm doing.

OASIS

Scorching sand
Blazing sun
Freezing nights
This desert,
Day without shade
No warm place at night
Empty dunes expand
Along the horizon…
Day after day
Night after night
This desolate land swings,
With wild extremes
Of ice and fire…
In this desert
Between life and death,
Water is the difference

In the distance
An oasis shimmers
For rest, strength…
I carry
All the water
I can,
Walk on
Not knowing of
A next oasis

At the edge
Of this desert
Infinite sand meets
Endless water…
Reaching this edge
Of all I've known
Life has been preparation
For this journey

ABOUT THE AUTHOR

One of Canada's most insightful writer's, Deborah Morrison is the author of ***Mystical Poetry*** and is co-author with Arvind Singh of the novel ***Nexus*** and the breakthrough non-fiction bestseller ***The Law of Attraction: Making it Work for You!***

The Hamilton Ontario-based writer is inspired by the healing power of the written word, nature and people. She's also a Psychotherapist/Counsellor, Early Childhood Educator, and Yoga Instructor.

She holds an Honours Degree in Religious Studies/ Sociology from McMaster University and has undertaken extensive research in Eastern and Western thought in the framework of contemporary and comparative studies. She has written several published articles on natural therapies, yoga, psychology and spirituality.

Deborah Morrison is a past executive member of the Tower Poetry Society of Hamilton, Ontario; the oldest poetry society in North America.

Deborah Morrison's poetical work ***In the Garden: Where Inspiration Grows*** is an imaginative and deeply inspirational collection of poetry. Varied aspects of the Garden are highlighted in unique, evocative, insightful ways from sacred earth, to flowers in wondrous full bloom, dreams manifested, creativity/motivational themes explored, and spirituality revealed.

Explore ***In the Garden: Where Inspiration Grows*** and discover the Garden as poetry of the Earth.